CLEO
ON THE MOVE

Caroline Mockford

Barefoot Books
Celebrating Art and Story

Cleo wakes,
Cleo winks.

Cleo yawns,
Cleo blinks.

Caspar sniffs,
Cleo frowns.

We're moving to another house.

It isn't far away.

...now you can
run and play!

Cleo dashes,
Caspar chases.

Cleo wins the race.

There's so much here
to see and smell,

For Ned and Joe — C. M.
For Felix — S. B.

Barefoot Books
124 Walcot Street
Bath BA1 5BG

Text copyright © 2002 by Stella Blackstone
Illustrations copyright © 2002 by Caroline Mockford
The moral right of Stella Blackstone to be identified as the author
and Caroline Mockford to be identified as the illustrator
of this work has been asserted

This book is printed on 100% acid-free paper
The illustrations were prepared in acrylics on 140lb watercolour paper
Design by Jennie Hoare, Bradford on Avon
Typeset in 44pt Providence Sans bold
Colour separation by Bright Arts Graphics, Singapore
Printed and bound in Singapore
by Tien Wah Press (Pte.) Ltd.

Hardback ISBN 1 84148 897 6

British Cataloguing-in-Publication Data:
a catalogue record for this book is
available from the British Library

1 3 5 7 9 8 6 4 2

Barefoot Books
Celebrating Art and Story

At Barefoot Books, we celebrate art and story with books that open the hearts and minds of children from all walks of life, inspiring them to read deeper, search further, and explore their own creative gifts. Taking our inspiration from many different cultures, we focus on themes that encourage independence of spirit, enthusiasm for learning, and acceptance of other traditions. Thoughtfully prepared by writers, artists, and storytellers from all over the world, our products combine the best of the present with the best of the past to educate our children as the caretakers of tomorrow.

www.barefootbooks.com